KYLIE THE MAGNIFICENT

KYLIE THE MAGNIFICENT

MARTY CHAN

ORCA BOOK PUBLISHERS

Published in Canada and the United States in 2021 by Orca Book Publishers.
orcabook.com

Library and Archives Canada Cataloguing in Publication
Title: Kylie the magnificent / Marty Chan.
Names: Chan, Marty, author.
Series: Orca currents.
Description: Series statement: Orca currents
Identifiers: Canadiana (print) 20210095164 | Canadiana (ebook) 20210095199 | ISBN 9781459828070 (softcover) | ISBN 9781459828087 (PDF) | ISBN 9781459828094 (EPUB)
Classification: LCC PS8555.H39244 K95 2021 | DDC jc813/.54—dc23

Library of Congress Control Number: 2020951493

Summary: In this high-interest accessible novel for middle-grade readers, amateur magician Kylie has to work hard to be taken seriously.

Orca Book Publishers is committed to reducing the consumption of nonrenewable resources in the making of our books. We make every effort to use materials that support a sustainable future.

Orca Book Publishers gratefully acknowledges the support for its publishing programs provided by the following agencies: the Government of Canada, the Canada Council for the Arts and the Province of British Columbia through the BC Arts Council and the Book Publishing Tax Credit.

Edited by Tanya Trafford
Design by Ella Collier
Cover artwork by Ella Collier
Author photo by Ryan Parker

Printed and bound in Canada.

24 23 22 21 • 1 2 3 4

To all the kids who chase the

dream of becoming magicians

Chapter One

"Magic is real. Not like in the *Harry Potter* movies. I'm talking about real magic, like what I'm about to show you." I was talking to myself, practicing what I was going to say onstage.

"Next!" a voice called. "Who's next?"

"Okay, Kylie," I muttered. "You've got this."

"I said *next!*" the voice boomed.

"Coming!" I yelled. I headed onto the stage.

The first round of tryouts for the magic club's talent show was packed. Every magician in the club wanted a chance to get onstage. I had joined the club just six months back, but I had already learned some pretty amazing tricks. I wanted people to ooh and aah with wonder at my magic. I wanted them to clap for my tricks. I wanted them to jump to their feet and cheer for me. But all that would have to wait. Right now I just wanted to puke.

So far I had only ever done this trick in front of my bathroom mirror. Now I had to do it in front of Peter, the show's director and head of the magic club. My nerves were getting the better of me. I had to hold my hands to keep them from shaking.

Peter looked up from his clipboard and grunted. "Well, the stage is yours, Kylie. Let's get going, shall we? I have a lot of acts to see today."

He headed off the stage and took a seat in the front row, clicking his pen over and over again as he waited for me to start.

I fumbled in the vest pocket of my black jacket and pulled out a solved Rubik's Cube. Each of the six sides of nine blocks was a solid color. *Here goes nothing.*

"Magic is the thing that is real," I began. "No, wait. Hold on. I messed up." I looked out into the rows of seats. "Can I start over?" I asked.

Peter sighed. "Relax, Kylie. Breathe."

I shoved the cube back into my pocket. "Magic is real," I said. "Not like in the *Harry Potter* movies. I'm talking about *real* magic, like what I'm about to show you."

I pulled the cube out again, but it flew out of my hand and hit the stage floor with a *thud.*

"You okay, Kylie?" Peter asked.

"I'm fine. Fine," I said. "Just a little nervous, I guess."

As I bent over to pick up the cube, my wand and a deck of cards flew out of my vest pocket. I scooped them up and stuffed everything back into the pocket.

"Oh right, the cube. Oops...sorry," I said as I reached into my pocket to pull out the cube again. Only this time I pulled out a pink bra.

Peter chuckled.

"Magic is real," I began again as I stuffed the bra back into my pocket. When I pulled my hand out this time, a stuffed bunny was hugging my wrist. I shook the bunny off, and it went flying across the stage. It smacked against the black curtain and stuck there.

Peter laughed.

"Magic is real," I said again. "Let me show you with this...this...hey, where is my Rubik's Cube?"

I spun around the stage, searching for the cube.

"Check your pocket," Peter said.

I pulled out my wand, the cards and the bra. Then I pulled out a giant pencil that stretched and stretched until it was six feet long. I tossed it behind me as I eyed the stuffed rabbit. I hopped over to the curtain and yanked the toy off. I turned around to show the audience—well, Peter—that the rabbit was holding the cube.

"Ah," I said, trying to pry the cube from the bunny. "Magic is real. Take this ordinary Rubik's Cube." The bunny wouldn't let go. Finally I ripped the cube away, along with one of the bunny's feet. The foot landed in Peter's lap.

"Heh, heh," I said. "Looks like you got a lucky rabbit's foot."

He smiled. I could tell he was figuring out now that all my fumbling was actually part of my act.

"But I won't need luck for this trick," I continued, really finding my groove. "For some people, this Rubik's Cube is just a kids' toy. But in the right hands, a toy can become a thing of magic."

I began to mix up the colors on the cube, twisting the various pieces this way and that.

Peter leaned forward. In the wings, some of the younger kids awaiting their turn were watching. I held up the cube, now a jumble of colors.

“They say it’s hard to solve this cube,” I said as I turned it over and over in my hand. “There are billions of patterns, and only one with solid colors on all six of its sides. It is almost impossible to solve. But in the world of magic, anything is possible.”

I tossed the cube up and caught it in one hand. I twisted my hand to reveal that all the sides were solid colors. Solved! The kids clapped, and I took a bow. Peter marked some notes on his clipboard. *Click, click, click* went his pen. I had no idea if he was impressed or not. All I could do was wait for him to speak.

After what seemed like an hour, he spoke. “Well, dear,” he said. He always called me *dear*, which I hated. “It’s not bad. But I’m not sure if your performance is right for the talent show.”

“You didn’t like my magic?” I asked.

He shook his head. “Oh, I liked it well enough. Your magic is solid. Solving a Rubik’s Cube that fast will wow the crowd. But if I had one note for you, it would be that you didn't let me, the audience, take a good look at the cube first. How do we know you didn't rig it to be solved quickly somehow?"

"I mixed up the cube in front of you," I said.

"Yes, but *you* were the one who did it," Peter said. "You didn't give me a chance to touch the cube."

"Okay, fair point. I'll keep that in mind for next time," I said. "Thank you."

"And the comedy bit at the beginning..." he added.

What about it? "It was funny, but I'm not sure if it's the right tone for you."

"What do you mean?" I asked.

"Don't get me wrong, dear. I love comedy magic when it's done right," Peter said. "The bunny toss made me laugh out loud."

"Thank you," I said.

"But I don't know. For one, your costume choice seems wrong. A suit jacket? That's for classic magicians like Blackstone. You should wear something that fits who you are. You know, like a dress. Maybe something sparkly," Peter said. "And it wouldn't hurt to put your hair up. You want to look pretty for your audience, dear."

I gritted my teeth and resisted telling him what I thought about his "advice." I wanted a spot in the show, but this guy was unbelievable.

"Well, I'd need a dress with pretty big pockets," I said, trying not to let him know how annoyed I was.

He ignored me, still rambling on with his thoughts. "Still, I suppose it would be good to have a girl in the show," he said. "For the optics, you know."

God. "So does that mean I'm in?" I asked.

Peter tapped his pen against the clipboard. "I don't know. Actual talent is the most important thing. We must maintain the integrity of the show. I only have one slot left for your age group, and still one more magician to try out. If he bombs, I'll consider you."

Gee, thanks. At least there was some hope. But it meant the next kid had to fail. An evil idea started to form in my brain. Maybe I could make them so nervous they'd mess up their trick. It was a bit underhanded, but I really wanted to be in the show.

"Who is the last magician to try out?" I asked, pretending I was just wondering.

Peter scanned his clipboard. "Let me see. Ah yes. Min-Jun is the last one in your age group."

"Min? Are you sure?" I asked.

Peter nodded.

My heart sank.

The kid who was up for the same slot as me was my best friend.

Chapter Two

I searched for Min backstage and wondered what I would say to him when I found him. Would I give him my support? Or would I try to crush his spirit? I honestly didn't know which way I would go.

I stopped to check out Dana Wynn as she worked on her act. Even though she was a couple of years older than me, she usually sat beside me at the meetings. We were the only girls in the club. She barely talked in the sessions. I think it was because she thought her braces made her sound weird. Anyway, she was a great magician.

Dana cut a rope in half, showed off the two ends, then brought them together and made the rope whole again.

I clapped. "Pretty awesome," I said. Peter never gave her—or me—any credit for our tricks. He only ever told us what we did wrong. I figured Dana should hear when she did something right.

"Almost perfect," she said, covering her mouth with one hand. "I'm still working on how to piece the rope together more smoothly."

"I didn't see anything weird," I said. "I think you were perfect."

"Thank you," Dana said. "I saw your act from the wings. Good job, Kylie. How did you do the thing with the cube?"

I grinned. "You know the club saying."

She nodded as we both said it at the same time. "Magicians never reveal their secrets."

We laughed. Peter made everyone in the club chant this at the start and finish of every club meeting.

"Good luck with your tryout," I said.

"Thank you," she said, smiling for a second before covering her mouth with her hand again.

I found Min in the hallway. He swept his shaggy black hair out of his face and held up a large silver dollar between his fingers. He placed the coin on the palm of his hand, then made a fist. When he opened his hand...*poof!* No silver dollar. Min was the best.

"Hey, Kylie," Min said. "How did your tryout go?"

"Pretty good," I said. "Just have to wait for Peter to decide."

He clapped his hand on my shoulder. "You'll get in for sure. How did the bunny bit work?" he asked.

"Great!" I said. "Thanks for the idea. Putting Velcro on the stuffie's belly helped it stick to the curtains."

"It's a funny gag. I laughed when you said you were going to do it," Min said.

"Are you ready for your tryout?" I asked.

"I'm okay with making the coin vanish, but I'm afraid I'm going to mess up my script. I just wish I could do the trick and never have to talk."

Min reached into his vest pocket, fished out the silver dollar and flipped it in the air. He was a great magician but a lousy talker. Even though it had been four years since he'd come here from Korea, he was always worried about his accent. It was barely noticeable.

If I wanted my friend to mess up his tryout, I knew how to do it. I just had to say, *I'm sorry, what did you say? I can't understand.*

The coin rolled across the back of Min's fingers as he went over his lines. "Have you ever heard about people not being able to hang on to their money? I'm one of those people." He took the coin from the back of his hand and placed it on his palm, closing his fingers over the silver dollar. With a snap of his fingers...*poof!* The coin was gone.

"How was that?" Min asked.

Here was my chance. With one question, I could make Min so nervous he'd screw up his tryout. One question...

Nah. I couldn't do it. Instead I forced a grin. "Fantastic. You're going to kill it with that act."

Min breathed a sigh of relief. "Thanks! Great to know you always have my back, Kylie."

"You'd better get to the stage. I think you might be next," I said.

"Will you stay and watch?" he asked.

"Wouldn't miss it." I couldn't believe I'd ever thought of messing with him. I could get another chance to be in the magic show. I couldn't get another friend like Min.

"Next!" Peter called out. "Min-Jun. You're next!"

"Good luck," I told Min, giving him two thumbs-up.

"Thanks," he said.

Min walked onstage and started his act. "Have-you-ever-heard-about-people-not-being-able-to-hang-on-to-their-money?" His entire act became one super-long sentence. I don't think he even stopped to take a breath.

But Min's coin magic was amazing. Even Peter gasped when Min reached under the paper on Peter's clipboard and produced the silver dollar he had made disappear a second earlier. If Min could have done the act without having to say a single word, it would have been pure magic.

Peter tapped his clipboard and stared at Min for what seemed like forever. "Well, I'm not sure. Great coin magic. No doubt about it. But you seemed nervous. You talked way too fast for anyone to understand."

"Sorry," Min said.

"I'm going to have to think about this," Peter said.

While I felt bad for my friend, I felt excited that I might still have a chance. I inched out onto the stage, hoping that if Peter saw me now, he'd cast me on the spot.

"Thank you for the chance to try out," Min said as he started to shuffle off.

"Keep working on your script," Peter said. "You just need to work on your patter. Talk a little slower. Maybe Kylie can give you some tips."

This was a good sign. I stepped forward, waiting for Peter to tell me that I was in the show.

"Well, maybe I don't need another act for the juniors," I heard Peter mutter to himself.

Gut punch. Peter's comment took the wind out of me. Had Min and I both lost our shot at the show? Min shambled toward me, looking like he had just lost his dog.

"Sorry, Min," I said. "I thought your magic was great. I couldn't see anything wrong with the coin trick."

"Thanks, Kylie. I wish I could be more like you. You're so natural onstage. Like, you're never scared or anything," Min said.

"Well, I wish I could have your skills," I said. "You are a real magician."

Min laughed. "Ha, too bad we can't be one person. Imagine a two-headed magician."

I chuckled. "Yeah, that would be something to... wait a minute."

Min cocked his head to the side. "What?"

His joke had given me an idea.

"Min," I said. "What if we could do an act together?"

"I don't know if there's a jacket big enough to fit us both," he said.

"No, not be one magician," I said. "I mean doing a two-person act."

He smiled. "That's not a bad idea. But didn't Peter say he only wanted solo acts for the show?"

"Maybe we can convince him to try something different," I said.

Min shook his head. "I don't know. He isn't really the type to change his mind. Do you you really think we could talk him into it?"

"Only one way to find out," I said. "Come on."

Chapter Three

Getting Peter to adjust his casting rule was going to be tough. Somehow I had to make him think that letting two people do one magic act was a good idea. Easier said than done. Peter loved to be in charge of everything and everybody. He had started the magic club, he ran the meetings, and he was putting together our talent show. He was the kind of guy who wanted everything done his way.

Then it hit me. I didn't have to make Peter think a two-person act was a good idea. I had to make him think it was *his* idea.

Dana was onstage in the middle of her rope act, but Peter seemed more interested in writing on his clipboard than watching her. I waited until she was done.

"Well, sweetie," Peter said, "it wasn't too bad, but I think you might want to work on your image a bit more. Have you thought about wearing more makeup?"

"Uh...what about the magic?" Dana asked.

"Yeah, well, I already have three other rope acts," Peter said. "I'll let you know."

"Um...thanks," Dana mumbled as she shuffled off the stage.

"Good job," I whispered as she walked past us.

She nodded, but her frown gave away how bad she felt.

Min followed me as I headed across the stage

and down the steps to Peter. I tried to get a peek at the lineup on his clipboard, but he caught me looking and placed his hands over the page.

"Yes?" he said. "May I help you?"

"Peter, you've been working so hard. Min and I were wondering if you need something to eat or drink."

"Well, that would be nice, dear," he said. "Since you asked, I would love an iced tea with some lemon wedges. The coffee shop down the street has the best tea. If you could be a dear and get me a large cup, that would be grand."

"Of course," I said. "Nothing to eat?"

"Oh, if it's not a bother, dear, a blueberry muffin with two pats of butter," Peter said as he started to make more notes on his clipboard. "No. Make that three pats. Butter. Not margarine. Butter."

Min tugged at the back of my jacket. "Ask him," he said.

"I'm working on it," I whispered.

Peter glanced up from his clipboard. "Next!" he called out.

I shifted over to block his view of the stage. "Peter, before we grab your iced tea and muffin, Min and I have a question. With so many solo acts, do you think the show might be running a little long?"

He stopped writing. "If I cast the show with the best magicians, the time will fly by."

"Oh yes," I said quickly. "I totally agree. You've always been able to pick out the brightest people. And I'm sure you're probably trying to work out ways to make sure the show doesn't slow down or get boring with the same kind of acts. You know, like having three rope tricks in the lineup?"

"Of course, dear," he said. "I'm always thinking of ways to shake things up."

"So I heard that you were thinking of putting in an act with two magicians," I said. "What a great idea. You're so smart."

Peter put his hand to his chin, like he was stroking a beard, then looked down at his clipboard. "Well, I didn't know word had gotten out, but that *is* something I have been thinking about."

Gotcha.

Min nudged me. "You know, Kylie and I have been working on a two-person act."

"I'm sure Peter's got some two-person acts lined up already," I said. I was really working it. "He's such a great director. He's always way ahead of the rest of us." I was laying it on thick.

Peter lowered his clipboard. "Hold on. Tell me more about your act. Who knows? I may have an opening."

Min and I glanced at each other. I hadn't really expected to get this far. I scrambled to come up with an idea. "It's an escape act," I said, making it up as I went along. "You know. Handcuffs. Shackles. Rope. The whole works."

Min grinned and nodded. "Yes, and we would get someone from the audience to check on the ropes."

Smart guy. He'd heard what Peter had said about my act.

Peter smiled. "Ooh, I like it. A nod to the great Harry Houdini. Kylie, I assume you'd be the lovely assistant who ties up Min?"

I bit my lip. "Um, well, why do *I* have to be the assistant?"

"Well, because that's the way it's always been done, dear," Peter replied.

"But didn't you say that a good magician always shakes things up? Keeps the audience on their toes?"

"Yes, yes, I might have said that," he agreed. "Tell you what. Show me what you've got and we'll go from there."

Uh-oh. Min jumped in. "We're still working out the details."

Peter made an irritating *tsk-tsk* noise. "Not ready? I'm sorry, but I'm only casting acts that are ready to go."

"There are still eight weeks until the show," I said. "What if we do our act for you in, let's say, a month? If you like it, you can cast us. If not, you still have time to find a substitute."

"Well, I don't know..." he said.

But I could tell he was wavering.

"Think about it. A Harry Houdini escape? No way anyone is going to top that," I said.

Peter sighed and scribbled some more on his clipboard. I would have loved to have seen what he was writing down. I was beginning to suspect it was all for show. "You have three weeks, dear," he said. "That's when I'll be conducting my last round of tryouts. If I like what I see, you're in. If not, I can always use someone with a pretty smile to take tickets," he said.

What a pig, I thought. But what I said to him was "Deal."

Later that day I watched Min dig through his box of magic. Silks. Playing cards. Coins. Silver linking rings. Sponge balls. Finally he fished out an old pair of handcuffs.

"Yes!" Min said. "I knew I had these somewhere. Kylie, help me put these on, will you?"

"I'm not going to be your assistant," I said.

Min looked at me. "*You* want to do the escape?"

"Why, you don't think I can?" I asked.

"Well, sure, I can teach you how, but you know I don't like talking in front of a crowd," Min said. "And I'd have to do a lot of talking to cover you while you do the escape."

"Min, this will be good practice for you. The more you talk in front of a crowd, the easier it will get."

"But you're a natural at acting and stuff. Me? I just like doing the magic," he said.

"So do I," I said as I grabbed the handcuffs. "You're the best magician I know, but you've got to get over your nerves and learn how to win over the crowd."

"I guess," Min said, pulling a large canvas sack from the box.

"What's that?" I asked.

"In the old days, this was a mailbag for letter carriers to lug the mail around in. Now it's the kind of thing magicians use for their escape acts," Min said.

"Really? How?"

"The magician is tied up and handcuffed and then climbs into the bag. It's big enough to cover the escape so no one can see how you get out," he explained.

"Awesome," I said. "Let's use it."

"Are you sure you don't want to be the assistant?" he asked again. "You're way better at entertaining the crowd."

I grabbed the mailbag from him. "Tell you what, Min. Teach me how to do the escape, and I'll come up with a little speech for you to deliver to the crowd. Deal?"

Min chewed his lower lip. He seemed pretty nervous. I only felt a little bad. But there was no way I was going to be the "lovely assistant."

Finally he stuck out his hand and said, "I'm in!"

Whew.

For the next week, Min patiently showed me over and over how to get out of the handcuffs and undo the ropes wrapped around me. I helped write a script for him. But even with my coaching, Min still had problems with the lines. While I fumbled with the ropes, he fumbled with his words. And boy, was he nervous. I mean, Min sweat so much I thought a waterfall was gushing from his armpits.

"Okay, I think I'm getting the hang of how to get out of the ropes," I said. "When do we get to the mailbag?"

Min waved his hand. "Let's save it for tomorrow. I really want to get these lines down."

"You don't have to remember them exactly, Min," I said. "Just get a sense of what you need to say and then wing it."

"But I have to time what I say with your actions so that everything is smooth," he pointed out.

I shook my head. "Not when we're still learning. Things can change, and you have to be able to roll with it."

"I have to get this part right. The lines have to be perfect," Min said, staring at the paper in his hand.

"Min, if you get too focused on the script, you're going to be uptight onstage." I had to figure out a way to help him relax. "You know what we need? An audience."

Min looked terrified. "What?" he asked. "*Now?* No way am I ready for a crowd."

"Just a trial run," I said. "It'll be fun. Plus, I think it will help calm you down."

"I'm not ready," he insisted. "*You're* not ready."

"Not a big crowd. Just your family. Mine. Maybe a couple of kids from school," I said.

"Forget it!" Min yelled. He looked angry now. "My parents would make me too nervous, and I don't want the kids at school to know what we're doing yet."

"Some strangers then?" I asked.

He shook his head. "No one. Not until we have everything locked down and perfect."

"Okay, okay," I said, holding up my hands. "Just relax, Min."

He stared down at his page and continued to practice his lines.

As I watched the sweat stains spread down his shirt from his armpits, I realized that Min would never feel like he was ready. The only way he would get over his nerves was if he had to do the show in front of a real live audience. I knew just the crowd he needed.

Chapter Four

My mom worked at a seniors' care home and was in charge of the social programming. The residents would make a perfect audience for our test run. They loved pretty much anyone. Show up, and they'd clap.

Now all I had to do was convince Mom to hire Min and me.

That night I helped make supper to get on her good side. She was making the vegetable dumplings that Lǎo Lao had taught her to cook. I liked my grandmother's better, but she lived in Shanghai. I missed her. Sometimes we talked, but she hated doing video chats. I chopped up the onions as Mom rolled out the dough. I wanted to make sure she was in a good mood before I popped the question.

"Just a little thinner, Kylie," she said.

"No problem, Mom. You need anything else chopped?"

"The carrots, but make sure you peel them first," Mom said.

"Okay, I'm on it."

I grabbed the carrots from the fridge.

Mom shook her head. "You know, I can't remember the last time you were this helpful."

"What do you mean? I help out all the time," I said.

She laughed. "No. I think I would remember."

"Last week I took out the garbage," I said.

"After I asked you eight times," she said. "Oh wait, *now* I remember the last time you helped without my asking. It was when you wanted to go off with your friends at the fair."

"Was it?" I asked. "I thought that was Dad's idea for us to go, since he was going to be busy working the booth all day."

My mom put her hands on her hips. "Kylie, out with it. While I enjoy your help, I don't want to wait for you to work up the nerve to ask. What do you want?"

"Okay, you got me," I admitted. "Min and I are working on a new magic act, but it kind of needs an audience. I was hoping we might be able to do it for the seniors at Sunrise."

"That's it?" Mom asked. "You want an audience?"

I nodded.

"Well, to tell you the truth, you'd be doing me a favor, Kylie. One of my singers canceled at the last minute, and I've been scrambling to find someone to fill in for her this Saturday. Do you think you and Min would be able to do two shows?"

"Two?" I asked.

"Yes, she was supposed to perform a morning and an afternoon show. Do you think you could do those slots? I can't pay you, but you'd be helping me out."

"You bet," I said. "We'll do them both."

This had certainly gone better than I had expected. Now that I had the audience, I had to somehow convince Min to do the shows.

The next day Min made me practice slipping out of the handcuffs while I ran through the script with him.

He paced around the room, chatting to an invisible crowd. He kept fumbling the lines. "The timer is ticking down. Will Kylie escape before the seven minutes is up? Or will she be bested by the handcuffs? No, wait. I meant before the clock runs out. Kylie, can I start over?"

I slipped my hand out of the cuffs. "Take it easy,

Min. You almost had it. Think about it this way. As the assistant, you're building the excitement. Don't worry about the exact lines."

"But I need to let you know how much time you have left," he said.

"I can barely hear you when I'm in the mailbag," I said. "Just focus on the crowd. Let them think time is running out."

"I can't remember if I say the line about the clock and then move back, or if I move back as I'm saying the line," he said. He shifted from one foot to the other as if the movement would help him remember.

"Min, look at me," I said. "It doesn't matter which foot you're on when you say the line as long as you say it."

"But I need to get this exactly right." He looked really panicky.

I freed my other hand from the cuffs. "Min, the audience doesn't know what you're supposed to do.

They won't care where you put your feet as long as you keep talking. Trust me."

"How do you know, Kylie?" he asked.

"I've done it before, Min. I've messed up tricks, but I've talked my way out of the mistake. If you trust in yourself, you can talk your way out of anything. As long as you don't admit you screwed up, the audience will think it's just a part of the act. Roll with it."

Min shook his head. "I'm sorry, but I'm not you."

I grabbed his hand. "Don't beat yourself up. You'll be great this Saturday."

His palm felt like it had sprung a leak. I had never known anyone to sweat so much. I let go and wiped my hand on my pants.

"Saturday? What's happening this weekend?" he asked.

"You know how you said you get nervous in front of a crowd?" I asked, trying to sound super cheery. "Well, I found a way to help you get over your nerves."

"What did you do, Kylie?" Min asked, his voice shaking.

"I found us an audience."

"No. I said no to a crowd until we're ready," he said. "And I'm totally not ready. Not even close."

"We have five days to get our act together," I said. "The deadline will force us to work harder. I'll be able to figure out the escape, and you'll learn your lines. And if we don't get it right during the first show, we'll be able to get it right for the second show."

"*Two* shows?!" Min shouted. "*Two shows?*"

"Yes, Min, two. Why, is that a problem?"

Min sagged to the floor and curled up like a baby. "I think I'm going to die," he moaned. "I can't do this. No way can I do this. I never should have agreed to this. I could have stuck to coin magic, but no, I had to try something new."

"Min, you're blowing this up bigger than it needs to be. You'll be great. We have plenty of time to get our act into shape. But we won't if you keep lying there. Get up, you baby." It was time for some tough love.

Slowly Min uncurled his body and climbed to his feet.

"You ready to run through the act again?" I asked.

He sighed. "Yes."

"Let's take it again from the part where I'm in the mailbag, okay?" I asked.

"Yeah," he said. "I'm just finishing off tying the top of the sack. And now I step over to the clock to start it."

I picked up the mailbag and held it in front of me, pretending I was inside it.

"The clock is counting down," Min said. "So I say, 'Kylie you have only seven minutes to escape. Seven minutes starting now.' Starting...now...now...why isn't the timer working? Oh, I forgot to turn it on. Let's back that up again."

Behind the mailbag, I started to worry that Min might never get it right. I wondered if I should put off our show at the care home to the following week.

"Okay, let me see if I can reset the timer," Min said, still messing up his lines. "Oh nuts, I set it for an hour. Hold on. Let's try this again. What? How? Why is the clock not working?"

I wondered if maybe we should put off our show to the following *year*.

Chapter Five

Nothing is more thrilling than watching the audience right before you're about to go onstage. I peeked through the crack in the door and spotted three seniors talking to each other as they took their seats at the front of the "stage," which was a wobbly riser on tiny metal legs. More residents were streaming in to find their seats. At the entrance to the dining hall, I could see my mom greeting everyone as they walked by.

I straightened my tux and checked on Min. He couldn't stop pacing around the office in his black suit. I had wanted to put him in a sparkly, flashy outfit like other magician's assistants. He'd shot down the idea and gone for a tuxedo too. He tugged nervously at the hem of the jacket.

"You're going to be great," I said, trying to calm him down.

"This is a bad idea," he said. "We should cancel."

I shook my head. "Too late, Min. They're all here."

The office door swung open. Mom stood in the doorway. "Are you ready?" she asked.

"Yes," I said.

Min doubled over and started panting. Mom looked at him and then at me. "Are you sure?"

"Min's ready too," I said. "Really. He'll be fine."

"Okay," she said. "Break a leg!"

Mom closed the door while I rubbed Min's back.

Outside the office door, I could hear her talking to the residents. "Okay, everyone, settle into your seats. We're about to get started. Trudy, that means you. Always the troublemaker."

The crowd laughed.

"Now you are in for a real treat. We all need a little magic in our lives, and today's performers are going to amaze you. They are marvelous, they are amazing, they are my daughter and her friend. Please put your hands together for Kylie and Min!"

The audience clapped.

"Showtime," I whispered. I had always wanted to say that.

I led the way into the dining hall. I hopped onto the riser and waved at Min to join me. He looked like he was ready to puke as he stepped up.

"Ladies and gentlemen," I boomed. "Prepare to be amazed. I, Kylie the Magnificent, will take you back to the time of Harry Houdini. The master of escapes!"

The crowed oohed.

Min whispered, "They're booing us."

I shook my head. "No, they're not. Just relax," I whispered. Then I put my show voice back on. "Ladies and gentlemen, I am going to attempt to perform an incredibly dangerous trick. My assistant, Min, will shackle me in handcuffs, tie me up with these ropes and chains, and put me into this giant mailbag. I will then attempt to escape in the time it takes for him to sing the national anthem."

The crowd laughed as Min shot me a glare. "I am *not* singing," he hissed. "Who said I was going to sing?"

"Sorry," I said, turning to the audience. "My assistant tells me he has a sore throat." The audience laughed. "Instead, we will use a timer. Now, Min, if you'll be so kind. Please tie me up."

Min began to wrap the ropes and chains around me. I puffed my arms out from my sides so that I could create some slack for later. He pulled a little tighter than he had done in the practice session. I guessed he didn't like my joke about him singing. The rope dug into my ribs.

"Easy there, Min," I said, faking a smile to the seniors.

The ladies in the front row laughed.

"We have to make sure the restraints are tight," Min said. "So that there's no possible way she can escape. And now..."

The crowd leaned forward as Min reached down into a box and pulled out a pair of handcuffs. The seniors oohed again.

"A pair of police handcuffs," Min said. "And the only key is right here." He held up the key for everyone to see before he placed it in his jacket pocket.

"I'm ready for anything you throw at me," I said.

Min slapped the handcuffs around my wrists and locked me up. Then he stepped back and turned to the crowd.

"There is no way she can possibly escape!" Min boomed. "But...but..."

He forgot his next line.

I jumped in. "But just to be sure, do you want him to tighten the ropes?"

"YES!" roared the crowd.

Min turned to me and mouthed, *Thanks.*

I nodded.

"You heard the audience, Kylie," he said, getting back on track with his lines.

Min stepped behind me and yanked on the ropes. I pretended I was in pain as he moved me back to the giant mailbag on the riser.

"And now I will be covered in this old mailbag," I said. "And...and...Min..." I tried to get him to say his next line.

Finally Min caught on. "Right. I will set the timer for seven minutes. Kylie must escape before the timer runs out, which is...starting *now*."

The crowd fell silent.

"Here we go," Min said as he pulled the sack up and over my head.

As soon as I was covered, I tried to get out of the ropes and chains. The slack I had created earlier made them loose enough to slip right off my body. Now the handcuffs. I hit the secret latch to open them, but it didn't work.

I tried a second time. Third. Fourth. Fifth. Nothing.

"Three minutes left!" Min announced.

I could hear the audience clapping and cheering, waiting for me to come out.

The latch wasn't working at all. I tried to escape, but the handcuffs were snug around my wrists and digging into my skin. Ow. Nothing I did was working and time was running out.

"How's it going in there?" Min asked.

"Good. I'm fine. Great," I said, grunting as I pulled at the cuffs.

"Ten seconds left, Kylie."

The crowd began to count down. "Nine...eight... seven..."

Forget the cuffs. I had to get out of the bag. I reached up to undo the knot, but the handcuffs made it hard for me to do anything.

"Four...three...two...one," the crowd chanted.

I was still stuck in the mailbag. The crowd laughed and then fell silent as I thrashed around.

"Um...nothing is wrong. Everything's perfectly fine!" Min shouted. "Just talk among yourselves while I...uh...I just have to check on one thing."

Nothing I could do would get the handcuffs off.

"What's going on?" Min whispered. "Get out of there."

"I can't," I said.

"Why not?" he asked.

"I'm still locked up," I said.

"We'll fix this in a minute," Min said to everyone.

The crowd grew quiet. I thought I might have heard someone cough.

"I'm really stuck," I hissed.

"Well, just flick the *you-know-what*," Min whispered.

"I told you, it's not working," I said.

"Just get out," he said.

I tried one more time to slip out of the handcuffs, but they remained tight around my wrists.

Min called out, "We've got this. Don't worry. Almost there."

No matter how hard I tried, I couldn't get out.

"It's no use," I said. "I can't do this."

Suddenly fresh air blasted the top of my head as the mailbag opened and slid down. Min glared at me. The seniors stared at us, not sure what to do next.

"Ta-*da*!" I said, showing off my cuffed wrists.

At the back of the room, Mom started to clap.

A few of the seniors joined in, but most began talking to each other instead.

"Nothing could be worse than this," I said to Min as the residents walked and wheeled their way out of the dining hall.

"I can think of something," he said.

"What?"

He stared at me and then said, "We have to do this all over again in an hour."

Chapter Six

Once the dining hall was empty, Min pulled out his key and unlocked the handcuffs.

"I'm telling you I couldn't make them work," I said as I rubbed my red wrists.

He slapped one cuff around his wrist and fiddled with the secret latch. It quickly popped open. He raised an eyebrow at me.

"Well, they didn't work when I was in the mailbag," I said.

"That's because you didn't practice enough," Min said. "You were too busy revising my script instead of learning what you need to do to make the trick work."

"I was trying to get you to relax, Min."

"No, you were messing with me, and you weren't paying attention," he said, his voice rising. "I told you we weren't ready, but did you listen? No."

I picked up the canvas sack and started to fold it up. "Sorry, Min. I wanted you to relax. You seemed so nervous onstage."

"That's not the problem," he said. "Failing to escape in an escape act—that's a problem."

"Is this about the singing? I promise I'll stick to the script next time," I said.

Min coiled up the rope. "No way, Kylie. We're not going through that again. No way. For the next show *I'm* doing the escape. You can be the assistant."

"You haven't given me a proper chance," I said. "I know I can do it, Min."

"We can try it again once you learn how to do the trick right. That time is not now. We can't risk another screwup in front of an audience," he said.

Mom approached us before I could say anything more. "Well, that was quite the performance," she said with a small smile. "I guess you're still working out the kinks?"

"We'll be much better for the next show, Mrs. Mah-Cardinal," Min said.

"You were perfectly fine," Mom said. She flashed her fake smile. When her teeth disappeared behind her thinned-out lips, I knew Mom was pretending. I remembered that fake smile from when Dad's old army buddy slept over at our house and caught Mom staring at the dirty socks he had put on the end table. He went to move them, but she said it was "perfectly fine" and flashed her thin-lipped *pretend* smile at Dad. Mom's fake smile was a pretty good sign that our show had sucked.

"Don't worry, Mom," I said. "Min's going to do the escape in the second show."

Her thin lips parted to reveal a toothy grin. "Well, if that's what you think you should do, I'm not one to stand in your way. You two know what's best for your show. I'll leave you to get ready."

I tossed Min the mailbag and stomped to the other side of the stage.

The second show didn't get off to a good start. As the magician, Min lacked the charm to win over the crowd. Some of the seniors in the second group stared out the dining-hall window as Min talked.

"Prepare to be taken to a world of wonder and magic. To the time of Harry Houdini," he said. "You will be filled with wonder. I mean, you will be filled with the wonder of the magic you'll see...today. This afternoon. Now."

Silence.

I had to win back the crowd. I scooped up the rope and stepped to the edge of the riser. "The Magnificent Min will attempt to escape from ropes, chains and the dreaded handcuffs. And to make it even harder for him, he'll do it all while being stuffed in this giant mailbag that stinks of old onions."

The seniors laughed. The ones who were staring out the window now turned to us.

"Yes, and my capable assistant will tie me up. Kylie, if you please," Min said.

"Capable?" I said.

"Yes."

"You mean amazing," I said.

"No. Capable," Min said, deadly serious.

I flashed a look to the seniors in the front row. They were chuckling.

"Now please tie me up and make sure the ropes are good and tight," Min said.

I wrapped him in the rope.

"Oh, don't you worry about that," I said. I winked at the audience. They laughed.

I tugged hard on the rope to tighten it around Min's arms. He doubled over as the rope dug into his stomach. The crowd loved it.

"Not so tight," Min said in a wheezy voice.

"Oh. Sorry," I said. I winked at the people in the front row. They cheered.

One man yelled, "Tighter!"

The crowd laughed. We had them back on our side. I wrapped Min in the chains and guided him to the riser so he could step into the mailbag. Then I held up the handcuffs and slapped them around Min's wrists.

"Do you want me to make the ropes tighter?" I asked the crowd.

"Yes!" they roared.

Min glared at me as I stepped beside him and pulled hard on the ropes. Then I knelt down and raised the mailbag up and over Min's head.

"This is my favorite part of the act," I told the audience. "Now I finally have the stage to myself."

The ladies in the second row nudged each other and laughed.

"Now to set the timer for seven minutes," I said. "Will the Magnificent Min be able to free himself before the timer runs out? We'll find out!"

I started the timer and stepped off the riser while Min struggled inside the mailbag to get free. I headed to the first row of seniors and started making small talk. "So how are you? Do you like the food here? If you don't, I know some people who know some people." I pointed to the back of the room at Mom, who laughed and waved me off.

Onstage, Min continued to struggle in the mailbag.

"You okay in there?" I asked.

"Almost. Almost," his muffled voice called out.

The crowd laughed again. Min continued to struggle. The timer had ticked off thirty seconds now.

"Okay then. Take your time. Now's my chance to be the star," I said.

The seniors clapped.

I reached into my jacket pocket and pulled out a deck of cards, then headed to a silver-haired woman in the front row. "What's your name, young lady?" I asked.

She laughed. "Margaret. They call me Mags."

"No, they call her late for dinner," an old man yelled from the back of the dining hall.

Everyone laughed.

"Well, she's right on time now," I said. "Mags, take a look at the cards." I fanned them out for her. "Pick a card. Any card."

She began to reach for a card.

"No. Not that one," I said, moving the cards away. "Pick another card."

Laughter from the crowd. Mags picked a card.

"Now tell me what the card is," I said.

She glanced at the card. "The ace of spades."

"Exactly. That's the card I knew you would pick," I said.

The audience laughed.

"No, seriously," I explained. "I knew that was the one she would pick." I fanned the faces of the cards to the audience. They were *all* the ace of spades.

Chuckles.

"Oh, I see you don't believe me," I said. "Okay, I know Mags was going to pick the ace of spades because she has been sitting on it the whole time. Mags, can you please stand up?"

I held out my hands to help Mags to her feet. As soon as she was up, the people behind her started to laugh, point and cheer.

"What's going on?" Mags asked.

I turned her around to show her backside to everyone in the dining hall. More laughs. I reached behind her and pulled off the ace of spades that was stuck to her butt. Now the audience clapped.

"I guess I got it right in the end," I said.

More laughs. I glanced at the timer. Twenty seconds left. Min was still doubled over in the mailbag. Something was wrong.

I jumped up onto the riser, kicking the timer face down so the crowd couldn't see that Min was about to fail.

"Oops. My bad," I said. "Hey, Min, how are you doing in there?"

"Almost," he said.

"That's what I used to say to my mom when I was a kid in potty training. Almost," I grunted.

The crowd howled.

"Take your time. I've got all the time in the world," I said.

I held a lady's silver watch in my hand.

"At least, I have someone's time," I joked, looking right at Mags.

I nodded at her to look at her wrist. I had to do it several times before she finally caught on.

Mags checked her wrist. "Wait! That's my watch."

The audience gasped and then broke into more laughter.

"It's mine now," I joked, pretending to pocket the watch.

They howled with laughter. I checked on Min. Still no progress. The escape wasn't going to work. I had to figure out a different way to end our act.

"Okay, I guess I can give it back," I said to Mags. "But first let's use it to time how long it will actually take Min to escape. I think I broke the timer when I kicked it over. Does your watch have a calendar function? Because this could take days."

The audience roared. They were loving everything I did.

"I can get out on my own," Min grunted from inside the sack. "Almost free...almost."

The mailbag finally opened, and Min stumbled out. He was free, but his wrists looked red and raw from the handcuffs still around his wrist.

Min wiped the sweat off his forehead and bowed. He cracked a weak smile and tried to hide his cuffed hands from the crowd. I stepped in front of him and blocked the view. The seniors roared and clapped.

"Thank you," I said. "Thank you."

I glanced back at Min. He was not happy.

Chapter Seven

As the seniors headed out of the dining hall, a few stopped to talk to me. Mags led the charge. She got so close I could smell what she had eaten for lunch. Tuna salad. Definitely tuna.

"Young lady, I wanted to tell you that I laughed so hard I might have peed a little," she said.

"Well, that's the first time someone's done that

during my show," I said. "Now you're sure you still have your watch?"

She checked her wrist and laughed. "Of all the acts your mother has brought in, you're my favorite."

"Really?" I said. "That's great. Thank you."

"My husband wanted to be a magician when he was younger, but he never got around to it. He bought all sorts of magic books. They're in storage. I can get my daughter to pull them out and give them to you if you're interested."

"That's so kind," I said.

"I'll get them to your mom," Mags said. "Keep it up. You're great."

The other residents nodded. Mags joined them and walked away. I hopped onstage to help Min get out of the handcuffs. He had the key in his hand, but he couldn't quite fit it into the lock. I grabbed the key from him and opened the cuffs.

"I don't understand what went wrong," he said.

"It's okay," I said. "It can happen to the best of us."

He tested the handcuffs, snapping them shut. "Not to me. I worked on the escape for months. I can get out of the cuffs in my sleep."

"I'll bet it was the same problem I had," I said. "Put them on me."

"Why?"

"I'll show you," I said.

He slapped the cuffs on my wrists. I squirmed and twisted, trying to hit the secret latch, but nothing happened when I flicked it.

"See?" I said. "They won't open."

The cuffs remained firmly around my wrists.

"It can't be broken," he said. "Try the latch again."

I flicked again. Nothing.

Min tried thumbing the latch. Again. And again. And again. By his tenth try, the cuffs finally opened.

"See?" I said. "The latch only works some of the time—it's totally random. That's why I couldn't get out of them the first time."

"I'm sorry, Kylie," Min said. "I thought you had messed up, but it was my handcuffs that were broken. I didn't mean to blame you."

"Doesn't matter, Min," I said.

"This is my fault. I should have tested the handcuffs before the show. I ruined everything."

"No," I said. "If it weren't for the broken cuffs, we wouldn't have found a new way to do the act."

"I knew that we weren't ready to go on. If we'd had another week to work on everything, I would have found out the latch was broken. Then we wouldn't have looked like idiots onstage."

"You're too hard on yourself," I said. "Don't you remember what Peter talked about at the magic club? You have to prepare outs in case things go wrong. And I came up with a new ending. And the seniors loved it. Didn't you hear them?"

"I was in the mailbag," he said. "I was too busy trying to get the cuffs to open."

"Trust me, they loved us," I said.

"But I didn't do the escape properly," he said. "How could they love us?"

"I wish you could have seen the crowd during the show. They were howling. We could have done anything and they would have cheered," I said.

Min grumbled, "Come on, we didn't have a proper ending. I didn't even escape. How on earth do you expect me to believe that the audience liked our act?"

"Did you hear Mags?" I asked.

He scrunched his face. "The woman who said she'd get you her husband's magic books?"

I nodded. "You heard what else she said, right? We were her favorite act."

"She probably knew that your mom is the manager here. She's sucking up so she can get another pudding cup or something," he said.

"You are the most stubborn..." I said, but I stopped myself. I didn't want to fight. "What's it going to take to convince you the audience loved us?"

"Nothing," Min said. "All I need to know is right here." He held up the broken handcuffs. "They hated me."

"Forget the cuffs," I said. "We have the makings of a great comedy magic act."

"I don't think I want to try out for the talent show anymore," he said.

"Don't give up now, Min. We can get new handcuffs so we can keep practicing."

Min shook his head. "Maybe it's better if we do separate acts," he said. "You are way better on your own, and I need more time to make sure I get the magic right."

Min turned the handcuffs over and over in his hands, as if twisting them could make them work again.

I had to do something. "If I convince you people liked our act," I said, "will you promise to keep working on it?"

"How are you going to do that?" he asked.

"I'll prove it to you," I said. "Follow me."

Chapter Eight

Min and I stood in Mom's office. She was on the phone. Min shuffled a deck of cards, something he always did when he was nervous. I leaned against the filing cabinet and flicked the dust off the leaves of Mom's fake plant.

Min leaned forward. "This isn't fair. Your mom will take your side no matter what we ask."

"No way," I said. "She's always been straight with me."

"Really? You're telling me that your mom is going to tell you that you suck at magic? Is that what you're saying?"

"Yes, Min. Remember what she said after the first show?"

He swung one half of the deck from the bottom onto the top with just one hand. "She said we had some kinks to work out, but she also said she trusted us to know what was best."

"See?" I said. "Mom told us we had a problem, just in a nice way. Trust me, she'll tell us the truth about the second show."

Min sighed. "I still think it sucked as bad as the first one."

"Not even close," I said. "The shows were as different as eggplant and pizza."

"Huh?" Min nearly dropped his cards.

"Which one would you rather eat?" I asked.

He mumbled, "Pizza."

I nodded. "And that's what the second show was to the seniors. Pizza."

Min said nothing. Instead he started spreading the cards in his hands again. His card fans were always so smooth and perfect. I had to admit I was a little bit jealous of his talent.

Finally Mom finished her phone call. She hung up and walked around the desk. "Kylie, Min. You two were fantastic," she said. "What you did was amazing. The residents loved it."

"Great," I said. "Which show did you like the best?"

"Be honest," Min added.

Mom sat on the edge of the desk. "Well, it's just my opinion, but I liked the second one. The first one? Um, let's just say you two bounced back from defeat."

Min stared at Mom, then back at me before he turned to Mom again.

"They *liked* the second show? Are you sure?" he asked.

She nodded. "I've hired a lot of acts over the years, and I've learned one thing about my group. They will let me know what they like and don't like. They don't have time to put up with bad performers. And I'm telling you that they loved the second show."

Min chewed his bottom lip. "Are you just saying that to make Kylie feel good?"

Mom laughed. "No, she bombed in the first show. You can make them laugh, sweetie, but Min having to rescue you out of that bag? Not very magical."

"Ouch," I said. "You could have put a little sugar on that lemon."

She gave me a hug. "You're tough. I know you can take it."

"What if she'd gotten the escape right?" Min asked. "I'll bet the seniors would have loved the first show then."

Mom smiled. "Hard to say, Min. Why do you ask?"

"Min doesn't think we did so hot in the second show," I explained.

"Go ask the seniors. They'll tell you. But if you ask me, the second time was great. It was entertaining and funny. I could probably line up more shows at some of the other homes. Just say the word, and I'll make the calls."

"Really?" I said. "That would be awe–"

Min cut me off. "We'll have to talk about it."

Mom shrugged. "You'd be a hit."

"We'll think about it," Min said. "Thanks for the offer."

He headed out of the office. I chased after him and grabbed him by the arm.

"Don't tell me you're walking away from the chance of a lifetime," I said.

"Your mom said we should talk to the seniors. I want to hear what they thought. Straight from the source."

"You heard what my mom said," I pointed out. "Don't you believe her?"

He crossed his arms. "A mom is always going to take the side of their kid. I have to know for sure. From people you don't know."

I sighed. "Okay, Min. Let's go ask some of them."

"Not the woman who's going to give you her husband's magic books either. I want someone you *didn't* talk to."

"Fine, fine. You can ask whoever you want," I said.

We headed out into the main living area. A few seniors were chatting near the entrance doors. Min walked right up to them and stared until they looked up.

A tall thin man smiled at us. "Oh, look, it's the magic kids."

Min cleared his throat. "Yes. Excuse me, but we were hoping to get some feedback on our shows. Did you see the one just now or the one before?"

"I saw the one just now. Abby was with me," the old man said.

The shorter woman nodded.

The lady in a wheelchair beside the pair said, "I saw the one before."

"Good," Min said. "What did you think of our shows?"

"You were good," the man said.

Abby grabbed my hand. "You were great!" She nodded at Min. "And you were really good too."

Min's shoulders slumped. "Thanks," he mumbled as he walked away.

I glanced at the lady in the wheelchair. She tried to look away.

"And you, ma'am? You said you saw the first show. What did you think of it?" I asked.

She paused for what seemed like forever. Finally she said, "I thought your costumes looked very nice."

"Anything else?" Min asked.

She cleared her throat. "I liked your hair too."

Ouch. That was not a great review. "Um...thanks," I said.

I chased after Min and caught up to him in the dining hall as he grabbed his suitcase of props.

"So?" I asked. "*Now* do you believe me? And my mom? And everyone else who loved the show?"

"I don't want to do the act," he said. "The handcuffs didn't work. The act sucked."

Min wasn't listening to anyone. Not to me. Not to Mom. Not to the seniors who'd raved about the show. He seemed so down on everything.

"Min, what's really bothering you?" I asked.

"I just don't like the act, that's all," he said.

"They loved us. They laughed all the way through."

Min shook his head. "Kylie, you're going by their laughs. We have no idea if they were laughing with us or at us."

"Why does that matter?" I asked.

He stared at me, his eyes wide. "I looked stupid in front of everyone," he said. "I hated it. They were laughing at me like I was a fool."

I hadn't thought about Min's feelings. I'd loved the spotlight so much I hadn't stopped to think about what it would cost my friend.

"I'm sorry, Min. I didn't want you to look bad," I said.

"You didn't have to make me look bad," he said. "I did that all on my own when I couldn't do the escape."

"You couldn't help it. The handcuffs broke at the worst time, that's all," I said. "And you still got out of the mailbag. That's way more than I did."

"But it robbed me of my 'wow' moment," he said.

"What?"

He explained, "You know that feeling you get when you pull off a trick perfectly? For a second, people believe magic is real. I didn't get that moment."

"But we can get another pair of handcuffs," I said. "Then we can have that cool ending that you want. You will get your 'wow' moment."

"No, Kylie," Min said. "I'm done."

"Don't quit on me," I begged. "We can rebuild the act, get new handcuffs, work out the hiccups."

Min shook his head. "It's not going to work."

"Mom said she can book us a show next week," I said. "That's another chance to get it right. I promise you I'll get you that 'wow' moment."

"Why does this matter so much to you?" he asked.

"You're not the only one who wants that 'wow' moment," I said. "At least you get it in the magic club when you show off your tricks. Peter's always picking apart what I do."

"I think your magic is awesome," Min said.

"I want to show everyone what I can do at the talent show," I said. "So Peter can shut up for once. Come on, Min. We'll practice. We'll only do the show for the seniors if we get the escape right twenty times in a row."

"Thirty," he said.

I nodded. "As many as it takes. Min, you know I'd never want you to look stupid onstage. You're my best friend."

"You promise?" he asked.

I clapped my hand on his shoulder. "I'd do anything for you. What do you say, Min?" I asked.

"Okay," Min said. "I'll give it a try. I'm in."

Chapter Nine

For the rest of the week, Min and I worked on our new act in my living room. The audience had loved it when I had to stall for time. But we had to figure out a way to make Min look less like a clown and more like a magician.

"How about this?" Min said. "You could tie some extra knots in the rope or pull out an extra chain to wrap me up in. Something I didn't expect."

I sat up on the couch, excited. "Ooh, I love that idea."

"Except...you're my assistant," he said. "Why would you do that to me?"

"I know!" I shouted. "Maybe we play off the idea of how you treat me as the assistant."

"What do you mean?"

"You know how in every big magic act, the magician gets all the glory?" I said. "But it's the assistant who does all the work. She prances around the stage in a sparkly dress, waving her arms around to distract people. And the magician doesn't even give her a name. He just calls her his *lovely* assistant."

"That's the way it's always been done," he said. "The assistant is the helper."

I shook my head. "They get treated like a prop. Maybe my character is sick and tired of being ignored. Now she wants the spotlight."

He jumped up from the couch. “Oh, I get it. You get to stick it to me for all the times I’ve taken you for granted.”

“Yeah, you won’t let me get my moment to shine,” I said. “You boss me around like I’m your lackey, and that’s why I get my revenge on you. An extra knot or two.”

“Or three!” Min said.

I beamed. “Exactly. Treat me the same way Peter does at the magic club. Like he’s talking down to a little kid every time he gives feedback.”

“Yeah, I’ve noticed that. You and Dana get it the worst.”

“Did you see how Peter talked down to her at the tryout?” I asked.

“Yeah. I felt bad for her,” Min said.

“I think we set up your character to be more like Peter right from the start, so I have a reason to mess up your escape.”

"But then I look like a jerk," he pointed out.

"Yes, but the audience will get on your side when I try to mess you up," I said. "They'll think I made it impossible for you to escape. That's why you'll look like a real magician when you get out."

"Okay, but do I have to be mean to you?" Min asked.

"The meaner, the better for the act. Just talk down to me. Pretend you're Peter talking to me or Dana."

"I guess I could try," he said. "Kylie, one question. How will the audience know that the extra knots aren't part of the regular act?"

"Well, while I'm tying you up, I can let the audience in on it. Maybe I can wink at them or roll my eyes when you talk down to me," I said. "Then, once you're inside the mailbag, I can tell everyone my master plan. About how you've treated me so badly, and this is my chance to get even."

“Maybe take it easy on me being the jerk,” Min said.

“Don’t you worry,” I said. “The more I want revenge on you, the better you’ll look when you escape.”

“I’m not so sure about this,” he said.

“Trust me. It’ll be great for the act. Now I just have to figure out what to do while you’re in the mailbag. I think stealing the watch worked last time. What do you think, Min? Do that one again?”

Min shook his head. “Don’t get me wrong, Kylie. It’s a great trick, but not everyone wears a watch. What’s your backup?”

“Oh yeah, I hadn’t thought about that. If no one’s wearing one, I can do the Rubik’s Cube instant solve.”

Min nodded. “I love that trick. Can you get someone in the crowd to mix the cube up?”

“I could do that, but I’d need a bag for the solve,”

I said. "I guess I could leave one by the timer. How much time do you want in the sack?"

"I guess enough time for you to do two tricks for the audience," Min said. "Any longer and the audience might get bored."

"Makes sense. I'll have to work the script so that I can set up either the watch or the cube trick at the same time. Oh, and I should also get in some digs at you for how you treated me as your *lovely* assistant," I said.

"Maybe stick to the idea that you always wanted to be the star of the show," he said.

I started to pace around the living room table as I came up with more script ideas. "No, I'll poke fun at your breath or how you never wash your tuxedo."

"Maybe tease me about how I'm never going to escape," Min said.

"Yeah. I could say you'll have to beg me to be set free."

"That's not bad," he said. "And I could ask if you did something weird to the rope or the handcuffs. To really sell the idea that you did something to screw me up."

"Me?" I said, now pretending we were doing the act. "Why on earth would you ever think I would mess with your escape?" I batted my eyes at Min. "After all, I'm your *lovely* assistant."

He played along. "Kylie! What did you do to the ropes?"

"Absolutely nothing," I said. "I'm sure you'll be able to get out. After all, you are Magnificent Min. Now, why don't you folks sit back and relax? It may take a while. In fact, let's kill time with a trick. Something I've always wanted to do."

Min clapped. "That's great. I love it."

I continued, pretending to talk to an invisible audience. "Don't mind the screaming coming from the mailbag. Min likes to hear himself talk. He's a legend when it comes to magic. He tells me so every single day. Every single hour of the day."

"Um, do you think that's a bit much, Kylie?"

"Hey, Magnificent Min," I said. "Do you remember that time you stuffed me in the box and sawed me in half? Well, this is for all the hours I had to spend in that cramped thing."

He shook his head. "Wait. I never did that."

"I know. Roll with it," I said. "It's part of our backstory."

"Oh, right," Min said.

"And when you had me swap places with the tiger?" I said. "I have scratch marks on my scratch marks. Well, this is my revenge."

"Okay, okay, I think you've got it," Min said.

"Hold on, Min," I said. "Do you know what would be really funny? If you came out in just your underwear."

"Um, why?" Min asked.

"Maybe while I was tying you up, I undid your belt," I said. "That would be hilarious."

He fell silent.

"Maybe we could get some boxers. You know, the one with hearts on them. What do you think, Min?"

"I think it's too much, Kylie," he said.

"No way. It's the perfect punch line, you coming out of the mailbag in your underwear," I said. "The audience will eat it up."

"Let's just stick with me doing the escape," he said.

"Come on," I said. "This will be your 'wow' moment. I'll build it up so the crowd will think there's no way you can escape...then ta-da! You're free."

"Not in my underwear," he said.

"Okay, okay, but definitely I want to build up how much I want to get revenge on you."

Min shrugged. "I think you've got more than enough material."

"No. Not even close," I said. "I can work in some of the things Peter has said to me. I want your character to be nasty."

"I really don't want to be that kind of guy," Min said.

"It's part of the act," I said. "I make you look like a jerk. And when I mess up your escape, you have to do some real magic to get out. The crowd is going to love it when you finally get free."

"Will they?" Min asked. "Or will they boo?"

"Hey, I'm just thinking of ways to give you the 'wow' moment."

He glared at me. "No you're not. Trust me. You're not." He grabbed his things and headed to the front door.

"Where are you going, Min?"

"I think you need to find a new partner," he said.

Chapter Ten

No Min. No escape act. No magic show. Well, not one with Min anyway. But the show had to go on. I decided to work up a solo act to test out on an audience. Maybe somehow I could convince Peter to give me another shot even if I was solo. Mom booked a gig for me. The singer who had pulled out on Mom had also bailed on someone else.

I knew things weren't going to go well when I showed up at the seniors' home. There was no riser. My stage area was sandwiched between a rolling cart of dirty dishes and the buffet station.

The host seemed nervous to stand in front of a crowd. He ran in front of the seated seniors and said, "Natalie couldn't make it this week. Here's Kylie. Enjoy!" Then he ran off to hide in the back.

"Thank you," I said as I pushed the cart of dirty dishes to the side.

The crowd looked confused when I stepped in front of them.

"Hey, where's your guitar?" a grumpy man asked from his wheelchair.

"Oh, I'm not a singer," I explained. "I'm going to do some magic for you."

A few of the ladies clapped.

The grumpy man crossed his arms over his

chest. "It's Saturday. We always get the pretty girl who sings on Saturdays."

Not a great start to my show, but I ignored him and launched into my act.

"As you can see, there is nothing in my hands," I said, flashing both of my open hands. "But if you believe that magic is real, then anything is possible. Just like this."

I closed my fist and held it up in the air while I reached into my closed hand with my fingers and pulled out a red silk.

One woman clapped. A few coughed.

The grumpy man yelled, "My grandson does that trick every time he visits me."

Some of the people around him tried to shush him but with no luck.

"What else you got for us?" he yelled.

"Ah, I see that you don't quite believe in magic yet, but trust me, you will," I said. "When you see this, you won't believe your eyes."

It was so quiet in the room that I could hear a woman at the back ask her friend, "When does Natalie come back?"

Her question threw me. Instead of going with a card trick, I went straight to the end of my act. I wanted to get out of the room as fast as I could.

"Behold! A regular Rubik's Cube," I said. "Something you might have played with when you were a kid."

"I know how that works," the grumpy man said. "You get your grandkid to solve it."

The audience chuckled.

"But I can solve it even faster. First, let me mix it up," I said.

My fingers were sweaty, and the cube slipped out of my hand, landing on the tiled floor. I scooped it up, but my wand and cards did not fall out like they were supposed to. In a panic, I started to mix up the cube pieces, but I arranged them in the wrong pattern. The trick wasn't going to work until I reset the cube to the right setup.

"Um, I will solve this cube in just a minute," I said.

"Peel the stickers off," the grumpy man said. "That's how I'd do it."

The crowd laughed.

Without anyone watching, I could solve the cube in five minutes. In front of the restless seniors, that five minutes stretched to seven and a half. When I finally solved it, most people were talking to each other and ignoring me. I took a half bow and got out of the place as fast as I could. I had failed. Hard.

I had to face the truth. Without Min, I had no act. There was no point pretending. I'd have to tell Peter that there was no act for the magic show tryout.

The following week was the final tryout session. I headed to the theater early so I could talk to Peter, but Min had beaten me there. Only he wasn't talking to Peter. He was doing our escape act with Dana Wynn.

She wore a sparkly silver dress and a puffy blond wig that sat sideways on her head. She wobbled on a pair of high-heeled shoes beside Min, who was now tied up in ropes and chains. He held up his hands, which were in cuffs.

"And now that I'm tied up, Dana will cover me with this giant mailbag and set the timer for seven minutes."

Dana bent over and grabbed the top of the mailbag. She lifted it up and over Min's head. Min spotted me and quickly looked the other way just before the sack covered his face. Dana tied off the top and walked to the timer at the edge of the stage.

"And now the Magnificent Min will attempt to get out before the timer runs out," she said. She sounded as nervous as a kid doing an oral book report.

Peter leaned forward. There was no music to cover the awful silence. Dana stared awkwardly from Peter to the timer. She called out each passing minute and then stood and watched the timer. There was no banter, no entertaining the audience. It was painful to watch.

Finally Dana shouted, "Thirty seconds left!"

The mailbag began to move more violently as Min thrashed about inside.

"Twenty seconds, Min," Dana said, picking up the timer.

"I'm stuck!" Min shouted, his voice muffled.

"Ten seconds!"

The bag hopped twice.

Dana counted down: "Five...four...three...two..."

The mailbag popped open and fell around Min's feet. He stepped out, holding the opened handcuffs in his right hand and one of the ropes in his left.

"One!" he shouted as he tossed both behind him.

Peter jumped to his feet and clapped. "Bravo! Excellent. Amazing."

Min grabbed Dana's hand, and they took a bow. He refused to even look my way.

Peter jumped up onstage and clapped. I strained to hear what he had to say.

"I love the way you honored Harry Houdini with the escape act," Peter said. "Dana, you could maybe talk some more while Min's in the bag. Or walk around and smile at the audience. Something to keep us entertained."

Min smiled. "We'll work on the script."

"Well then, I think I have the final act for my talent show," said Peter.

My face felt hot. My best friend had just stolen my idea.

Chapter Eleven

Min nearly sprinted off the stage, leaving Dana to clear the props. I had to talk to him. A few magicians were warming up backstage and getting ready for their tryouts. One guy made a dove appear in his hands. Another teen spun a smartphone on his finger like a basketball. Min slipped past them and headed into the boys' washroom.

Like that was going to stop me.

"Coming in," I announced, shoving the bathroom door open.

Inside, two kids watched themselves in the mirror as they practiced their tricks. A curly-haired kid made a red sponge ball disappear, while his freckled friend pulled fake flowers out of his sleeve. They both gasped when they saw me.

"This is the boys' room," the freckle-faced kid whined.

I ignored them, making my way to the stalls. I could see Min's black dress shoes under the closed door of the last stall in the bathroom.

Bang, bang, bang! I slapped my hand against the metal door. "I know you're in there, Min. I can see your feet."

The two kids scrambled out of the room.

"Um...I'm busy right now," Min said.

"Get out here right now," I ordered. "I want to know why you stole my idea."

The stall door swung open. Min charged out. "*Your* idea?!"

"Yes, it was my idea," I said.

"No, it's *my* escape act," he pointed out. "I taught you how to do the escape. You had no idea how anything worked until I showed you."

"I was the one who came up with the assistant bit," I said.

His face turned bright red. "I did not use any of the script you came up with. All Dana did was count down the time. It's the way the trick has always been done. The classic way. The right way!"

"*What*?" I said. "That is a terrible way to do it."

"She's building the drama of the countdown."

"So she's a talking clock," I said. "She's a prop. Nothing more."

He crossed his arms over his chest. "How is that any better than what you had me doing?"

"What are you talking about?" I asked. "You got to be the magician."

Min shook his head. "You got to perform your tricks while you made me look bad in the mailbag. First you wanted me to look like a fool who didn't know how to get out. Then you wanted me to act like a jerk who deserved to fail. Then you wanted me to come out in my underwear! How is that fair?"

I glared at him.

Min kept ranting. "You wanted to look good. You wanted to be the star. You never stopped to think about what *I* wanted."

"That's no excuse to steal my idea and replace me with Dana," I said.

"You took away my 'wow' moment. All I wanted to do was show off my magic, and you turned me into a joke."

Min wiped his eyes with the sleeve of his tuxedo.

"You just had Dana counting down the timer," I said.

"If you had watched our act from the start, you would have seen that Dana was the one who set up the escape. She wasn't just a girl in a sparkly dress."

"I came in late," I said.

"Well, if you had seen everything, you'd know that I gave Dana a chance to shine in the show as well," Min said. "And she didn't have to put me down to get it. I treated her better than you treated me."

His comment hit hard. I'd wanted to build a comedy act so much I'd forgotten that it wasn't just a comedy act. It wasn't just a magic act. It was a chance to do something fun with my best friend.

"Min...I'm sorry. I got lost in the moment," I said.

He glared at me for the longest time, saying nothing.

A knock at the door.

"Um, are you guys done in there?" a boy asked through the door. "'Cause I really have to go."

"Yes, I'm done," I said. "Min, I am sorry for everything."

I headed to the door and pulled it open. *Whoosh.* The curly-haired kid pushed by me as he waddled to the stalls with his legs squeezed together.

I stopped and looked back at Min. "Break a leg at the show," I said.

"Thanks," he mumbled.

I headed into the backstage area. This year's talent show was a bust for me. Getting no stage time was going to sting. No friend was worse. I'd lost sight of what really mattered, and I only had myself to blame.

"Wait!"

I turned around. Min was walking toward me. I couldn't tell if he was going to yell at me or cry.

"Kylie, you know I'd never steal your idea," he said. "You're my friend."

"Still?" I asked.

He nodded. "Even when you're being a jerk."

"I was being a jerk—you're right," I said. "I'm sorry for what I did. I guess I wanted to show

Peter that I could be as good as anyone else in the club."

"I know you're good," Min said. "And I've heard a lot of the other club members say the same thing. And you saw the crowd at the seniors' home. Does Peter's opinion really matter anymore?"

It didn't. Min was absolutely right. It really didn't.

"Kylie, I have a new idea about our act," Min said. "If you're still interested in doing it."

I raised an eyebrow. "You sure? I don't want to kick Dana out."

"No. She'll still be in the act. And we can all have our 'wow' moment."

"Go on," I said. "I'm listening."

Chapter Twelve

Eager families packed the theater to watch their kids perform in the magic show. I peeked through a break in the black curtains and searched the audience for my parents. There they were, sitting in the front row.

Mom talked to Min's dad in the second row while my dad stared at his phone. Min's entire family filled the second row as well as part of the third. They looked pretty excited for the show to start.

Min paced back and forth as he went over his lines. Dana followed in his footsteps, also rehearsing her lines. She wore the same type of suit as Min and me. Not a whiff of a sparkly dress anywhere.

Dana stepped over a metal bucket in the middle of the floor. I wondered if Min or Dana had brought it in case one of them needed to throw up. My money was on Dana puking. She looked greener than Min did.

I stopped them from pacing.

"Breathe," I said. "Just breathe."

Min gritted his teeth. "I think I'm going to pass out."

"Me first," Dana said.

"No one's going to pass out. You're both going to knock them dead. Now straighten your tux, Min. And Dana, you've got some crud on your shoulder."

They fixed their costumes as I turned around to watch the kid onstage pull a silk out of his fist. The audience clapped loudly for him, and the boy took a bow.

Peter stepped onstage from the other side. "Yes. One more round of applause for the Magnificent Justin."

Hearing his stage name (geez, did every kid use "magnificent"?) made me think about how I hadn't been very magnificent to my friend. I was so glad we had worked things out.

"Thank you, Justin," Peter said, nodding toward the wings for Justin to leave.

Justin kept bowing until Peter gently pushed him off the stage. The audience laughed.

"Aaaaaaaand now for something truly special," Peter said. "We are going to turn back the calendar to the years of the great Harry Houdini. Ladies and gentlemen, put your hands together for our very own escape artist—the Magnificent Min and his two lovely assistants!"

Dana and I rolled our eyes at each other.

"That's our cue, Min," I said. "Go."

"I can't. My legs won't work," he said.

"Mine too," Dana said.

I shoved Min and Dana in front of me and stepped onto the stage.

"Good evening," I said. "My name is Kylie, and this is Dana. We are more than *lovely* assistants. We are magicians as well. And tonight you are in for a magical journey to the impossible," I said, glancing at Dana to prompt her to say her line.

Right on cue, she boomed, "Prepare to be amazed!"

Min looked at me. I nodded. He stepped forward. "I, Min the Magnificent, will attempt to free myself. I doubt even Harry Houdini himself could escape these bonds. My partners in magic, Dana and Kylie, will restrain me."

Oohs filled the theater as Dana and I wrapped Min up in the ropes and chains. Dana bumped into me as she circled around Min. She dropped the rope.

"Oops," she said. "Sorry."

The audience laughed. Min frowned.

"Dana and Kylie will do a better job of tying me up. Or else I'll have to replace them with someone who knows what they're doing," he said.

Dana and I glared at Min.

"Well? I'm waiting," he said.

I gave Dana a quick nod. "Don't worry, Min. We'll make sure you're tied up good and tight."

This got a chuckle from the audience. They let out a laugh when Dana tugged hard on the rope and Min started to gasp.

"Maybe not that tight," he said.

"Tighter?" Dana asked. "Okay."

The audience laughed louder as Min doubled over and moaned.

"Oh, are you okay?" I asked. "Are we not doing it right?"

He grunted. "It's fine. I'm good. Keep going."

Once we had him tied up and cuffed, Dana and I lifted the mailbag up and over Min's head.

I ran to the edge of the stage to pick up the timer. "We will set the time for seven minutes and see if the Magnificent Min can escape before the timer runs—" I stopped and glanced at Dana.

"What's wrong?"

"Seven minutes seems too easy, doesn't it?" I asked. "How about we set this thing for five minutes? Would you all like that?"

The audience cheered.

"What?" Min shouted from inside the sack. "No! That's not what we planned."

The crowd laughed.

Dana cracked a grin. "He says no. Make it three minutes."

"That's not what I said!" Min shouted from inside the sack.

"I have an even better idea," I said. "What if I try to do a magic trick with..." I reached into my pocket and pulled out my Rubik's Cube. "Let's see if the Magnificent Min can escape before I solve this puzzle."

I mixed up the colors on the cube and showed it to the audience. Then, with a flick of the wrist, I solved the cube instantly.

The audience howled and clapped.

"What do you say, O great magician?" I asked.

"Stick to the timer!" Min yelled from inside the mailbag.

Dana cupped her ear close to the bag. "He said he will go for it. And if you solve it before he gets out, he'll buy everyone an ice-cream cone."

"I did not say that!" Min's muffled voice screamed.

"Sorry," Dana said. "*Two* ice-cream cones."

"Nooooo!" he yelled.

The audience was loving every minute.

"Then shall we get started?" I asked. "Audience, give me a countdown from three...two..."

"One!" the crowd roared.

Behind me, Min hopped around inside the giant mailbag. I took my time mixing up the colors on the cube. Yawned. Then I mixed it up some more. The audience howled as I checked my watch.

"Ow, ow, ow!" Min shouted from inside the sack. "I think I broke my arm."

Dana looked across the stage at me, her eyes wide with panic. "Something's wrong!" she said.

"What? Min! Are you okay?" I asked.

"Help me open the mailbag, Kylie!" Dana shouted as she stepped behind Min.

I reached up to the top of the sack as it stretched out and blocked the audience's view of Dana. I worked at trying to undo the knot at the top, but it wasn't budging. I turned to the audience.

"Nothing to worry about," I said, my voice wobbling. "I'm sure he's fine."

The audience fell silent. I tried again to undo the knot.

"Dana! Can you get it on your side?" I asked frantically.

Suddenly the mailbag fell to the floor. I stepped back to reveal that Min was free and Dana was now the one completely tied up in ropes and chains. Her wrists were cuffed in front of her.

The audience burst into applause. Min stepped to the front of the stage and enjoyed his "wow" moment. We had created the perfect blend of comedy and magic. The audience roared.

Min and I took our bows and ran off the stage.

"Uh...guys...hello?" Dana said. "I'm still here."

The audience laughed.

Min and I rushed back onstage. We lifted the sack over Dana for a second, then dropped it. She stepped out, completely free of the ropes and chains. The audience jumped to their feet and applauded so loudly I couldn't even hear Min thanking everyone.

The three of us grabbed hands and took our final bow. Offstage, Peter raised his eyebrows, impressed.

We walked toward him.

He looked from Min to me to Dana. "That was incredible," he said, shaking his head. He reached out a hand to Min. "Well, Min, let me congratulate you on a fantastic and highly entertaining magic trick."

"Thanks," Min said, waving off Peter's hand and pointing at me. "But it was all Kylie's idea." That surprised me. It had been *his* idea for us all to have our "wow" moment. And then we had all worked together to make it happen. But it was worth taking the credit just to see Peter's face.

His mouth dropped open. "*You*? How did you come up with such a great idea?"

I glanced at my partners before turning to Peter.

"You know the old saying. A magician never reveals their secrets."

Acknowledgments

This book would not have been possible without the happy meeting of an incredibly talented (and "just normal") actor who went on to become a fantastic magician. Thank you, Billy Kidd, for showing us that the world of magic doesn't have to be an old boys' club. Also, thank you to Michelle Chan and Wei Wong, for helping me close my windows and end with clean hands.

DON'T MISS OUT ON MORE GREAT READS BY MARTY CHAN!

TD SUMMER READS SELECTION

CCBC BEST BOOKS FOR KIDS & TEENS

Everyone assumes that because he's Chinese, Jon Wong must be a first-class nerd who's good at math. So when a rumor starts that Jon is a kung fu master, rather than correct the mistake, Jon plays up the role and enjoys all the attention. But when the school bully challenges him to prove his skills, Jon must figure out a way to somehow keep his status as the cool kid. Without getting pulverized.

"AN IMMERSIVE PAGE-TURNING GHOST HUNT."
—Kirkus Reviews

Xander thinks the George Wickerman Hospital would be the perfect setting for Spirits and Specters, a role-playing game where players search for evidence of paranormal activities. According to local legend, ghosts walk the hallways of this now-abandoned building. What better location to go ghost hunting? Even though they didn't really believe the rumors, Xander and his friends soon begin to suspect that they are not alone. Is this place actually haunted by ghosts? Or something even more terrifying?

Marty Chan is an award-winning author of dozens of books for kids, including *Kung Fu Master* and *Haunted Hospital* in the Orca Currents line and the award-winning Marty Chan Mystery series. He tours schools and libraries across Canada, using storytelling, stage magic and improv to ignite a passion in kids for reading. He lives in Edmonton.

orca currents